THE VIRGIN AND THE Vixen

ELIANA PIERS

The Virgin and the Vixen is a work of fiction. Names, characters, places, and incidents are the products of the author's imagination or are used fictitiously. Any resemblance to actual events, locales, or persons, living or dead, is entirely coincidental.

ISBN E-Book 978-1-998281-08-4
ISBN Print 978-1-998281-09-1

To The One

Free E-book

Get my **FREE** Short Story when you sign up to join my mailing list. Plus you'll learn more about me, get sneak peeks at what's in the works, as well as receive access to some discounted or free books from other authors.

Sweeten the Rogue: One wager, one evening of passion, two possible futures for a rogue and a lady

Or use this link here to receive the free ebook: https://bit.ly/SweetenTheRogue

Or email me to get the story: elianapiers@gmail.com

Contents

Author's Note

Hello Beautiful Reader,

Welcome to the Beau Monde. Most, if not all, of my books are part of an interconnected world with the Good Dukes, where it all started. This series, The Ashbourne Legacy follows the 7 brothers of Snow White, and it has some enchanting fairytale vibes for you.

If you like SWEET & SPICY, you are in for a treat.

I love to write funny, easy, breezy stories where the characters learn things about themselves and the world around them, all the while continuing to reach for hope, joy, and above all, LOVE.

Love always wins. Love never fails.

You will always read a happy ending in my stories.

I write to have fun, and so I make stories fit into a historical context, but I often take leeway with history. SO, if you are looking for a 100% accurate depiction of historical language and settings, please put this book down. You will be disappointed. And I don't want that. You don't want that. Neither of us wants you to be disappointed. Let's just be happy. The world is a hard enough place as it is.

IF, however, you don't mind to sacrifice some historical truths in the name of LOVE and HUMOR, AND you want to read about some HOT men falling head over heels in love with some INTELLIGENT, STRONG, INDEPENDENT women, then read on, dear reader.

Much love,

Eliana Piers

Chapter 1

1816 England

"HEART OF GOLD I tell you," the dowager duchess of Whitewood chuckled. "I'm not biased in the least." She shook out the leaves in her hands as she replaced them in the vase. "Of course I know he's my son, but he's one of seven, and I don't say the same thing about all my sons." She sent a coy smile to Della. "Heart of gold. Wouldn't you agree?"

One thousand percent Lady Della, daughter to The Earl of Woburn, agreed. But she had to taper her agreement. She would feel foolish gushing about her love for Mavis' third son, no matter how long she had known and loved the dowager. Being neighbors made their families close, but she wasn't willing to divulge just how close. Especially to the mother of the man she had loved her entire life. Or at least since he gave her a fish for her eighth birthday. It was the only pet her parents would allow her to keep. Until now.

No, she wasn't willing to share her heart. Besides, her and her heart had just had a heart to heart this morning about how they would no longer pine after the boy-turned-man with a heart of gold. No matter how broad his shoulders were. No matter how enticing he looked when he raked his hands through his hair. And, in particular today, no matter how charming he was when he was hosting his annual garden party to encourage the *ton* to adopt a pet in need.

She groaned. Today, he would be exceedingly charming. There was no denying it. But she could start to deny her heart and move on. Plenty of women experienced unrequited love. She wasn't the only woman on the planet who would drop to her knees for a man who didn't love her. But between being a woman who managed or mismanaged one-sided love, she was going to be a woman who managed it well. Starting now.

"Are you alright?" Mavis asked.

"Yes, of course. Why do you ask?"

"I thought I heard you...groan." Mavis looked around at the tables and chairs set up. "It's quite the load for you to plan this event every year. Perhaps you're growing tired of it?"

Della hadn't realized she sighed aloud. She would have to watch herself. "I love this event. Your son truly does have a heart of gold. To place all these animals in loving homes proves it."

"Well, I have to agree. Obviously." She winked at Della. "If only he wasn't quite so bashful, perhaps he could convince people to donate more. When he comes home just before the garden party, I mean to ask him if he'll finally give a speech this year." Mavis patted Della's hand. "He's lucky to have you."

If only he did have her.

"If it weren't for your eager and creative mind to plan this event, he probably would have discontinued it long ago."

"He may be quiet, but if he wants something, he goes after it." And that's how Della knew, Colin wasn't interested in her. He was shy. But he was determined. He was the kind of man who knew how to make things happen. Della could only wish he would make things happen with her.

"I'm not so sure." Mavis hummed out the phrase. There was an unexpected bumbling silence as Mavis fiddled with some more flowers in another vase. Picking one daisy out of the bunch, she pointed it at Della. It bounced in the air a couple of times. "He hasn't gone after you yet."

Della balked at the suggestion. Mavis had never explicitly pointed this out before. Over all the years, all the visits, all the kerfuffles, all the madness of so many children playing together, the topic of Della and Colin had not once arisen. At least, between Mavis and Della. Her tongue was stuck to the roof of her mouth as if honey from her tea was gluing it in place. With some prompting, Della freed her tongue. "We're just friends. I see him as only a friend. A wonderful friend, he is. A friend for the ages." She should have stopped before *the ages* sentence. It was already enough *friends,* nevermind how ridiculous the last sentence sounded.

Apparently Mavis wanted to clarify the fourfold usage of the word *friends*. "Just friends?"

"Yes." Della nodded her head emphatically. Then jerked her head down once and bobbed it back up. That should do it. That should convince the mother of her best friend that she wasn't in love with him.

***

Just friends. Colin pursed his lips. Well, that was that then. He had his answer. She had said it at least four times.

For some reason he had thought it would hurt more. He just stood as still as a tree available for any bird to come perch upon. But apparently no bird wanted to perch itself on his branches.

Standing on the terrace just outside his bedroom, Colin had only intended on checking the weather. Eavesdropping was not on his agenda.

He had had only two intentions today. The first was to do a quick test flight with his new homing pigeons to see if they would actually return home. The second was to tell his best friend that he loved her.

Plan two was off the list now that he knew how she felt.

A pang sliced through his heart. It was delayed. It should have stung when he first heard the words, but the shock had numbed him. He wasn't prepared to hear her declaration of friendship. Despite knowing they were friends. So now, upon further reflection of her announcement, he found his heart quite...heavy. A touch lethargic. The beating felt a bit like a woodpecker chipping away at bark, only he wasn't getting any food, his heart was just banging itself on the shell of his body. Over and over again. No reprieve. No reward.

It had been an audacious plan, truth be told. Nothing like Colin would normally undertake. And before this summer, whenever he had weighed the risks, caution won. He wanted to keep Della as a friend. He couldn't tell her how he felt. How he loved the way her nose crinkled whenever a dog bounded over to her to be stroked. Or how he was in awe of her abilities to manage people and events in a way that stressed him beyond belief. Or how he always watched her leave a room because, well, he couldn't help watching the sway of her bottom. Just one more time.

It was not like him to be so bold. It was not like him to be bold at all, really.

But after his two older brothers, Arthur and Barnaby, had shared the news of their engagements within weeks of each other, he figured it was time to shoot his shot. Perhaps fate was doling out betrothals to the Ashbournes this summer. Perhaps he could slide through thirty plus years without pursuing a woman and secure the only one he had ever dreamed of far too many times. Perhaps...but no.

He had hoped–he cut himself off. It was too much self-pity. He had to clear his mind.

Might as well proceed with plan one. The test flight still needed to be done. He wanted to see if perhaps there was an easy way to communicate between the Ashbourne mines using pigeons to carry messages. Only a few select people knew of his idea. He wasn't ready to share it with all seven brothers and one sister just yet.

Though they all bowed to him as the animal-whisperer, he wasn't ready to take on a new role until he had tested it thoroughly. He was content about his advancements with the canaries in the mines. He ensured miners carried oxygen packs on their person to revive any birds that should pass out from toxins released into the air. So far the plan was working. He wanted to have the same success with the pigeons. If possible.

Pigeons were the perfect distraction from love.

Full of resolve, Colin left the terrace, head held high, despite the weight on his shoulders. Once he arrived at the dovecote, he gently took out one of the pigeons he had been training. Hopefully this trial flight would work and the pigeon would return home. It could be quite an effective way of sending messages.

Messages. The word lodged itself in his mind. A visual filled his mind. Message carried by a pigeon soaring through blue skies scattered with clouds reaching to the heavens. A message to the heavens. To fate.

He had thought he needed to let go of his silly notion of fate. But in that moment, he realized that by divulging his feelings to Della, he wasn't truly trusting fate. Telling her so directly was him taking fate into his own hands. Surely it was time to actually trust fate. He had heard of messages being cast in bottles. Well, he had no bottles and no oceans. But he had his pigeon and the sky.

Colin grabbed a piece of foolscap sheltered beside the dovecote, ready for future messages. The future was now. In large block letters, he wrote:

SEND LOVE.

Chapter 2

DELLA CHIDED HERSELF ON feeling guilty for lying to Mavis. Well, she hadn't lied. She was telling her a future truth. *A future truth? Really, Della. Be better. You are better than that. And if you're not, then be better than that.*

It was difficult to argue with oneself. And tiring. Della straightened another chair. She wanted this event to be perfect. She had no idea why. Alright, that was another lie. She knew exactly why she wanted the event to be perfect. If the event was a success, Colin would reward her with a hug.

She sighed. Hugs on her mind, she put her arms around herself, imagining Colin. The warmth. The solid wall of muscle. The graze of his chin into her hair and across her temple. She could practically smell him right now. Bergamot and pine. He was always outside. If she couldn't find him outside though, he was probably reading or making notes on new ways to work with one of the many animals he usually had around him. He was so clever. And kind. She sighed again. Truly, his hugs were what she lived for.

Not anymore though. This event did not have to be perfect. She did not need that hug. Della pushed the chair to be at an awkward angle. There, that should do it. Not perfect.

The sun was hot. Perhaps it was getting to her. She took a moment to stand underneath a nearby tree to grab some shade. Looking up into the branches she recalled climbing trees with Colin and his brothers. Summer especially held the best memories. She leaned her head against the trunk of the tree and closed her eyes.

He did have a heart of gold. And a shy smile that warmed her heart because she knew that he didn't fake those kinds of things. When he looked at her, he truly saw her. He knew her secrets. Including the secret desire to become some kind of event planner for the *beau monde*. Knowing that secret was at least part of the reason why he continued allowing her to plan this annual event for him. His heart. His smile. Those arms. She didn't have to see him to visualize the shoulders on that man. And his biceps. She could feel them now, wrapping around her in a hug that she never wanted to dissolve.

A branch overhead rustled. Glancing up, she observed a bird perched on a branch. It flickered its head side to side. She squinted, trying to peer more closely at the bird. Something was stuck on its leg. Wishing she could unstick the item from its leg, she watched it tap its leg up and down several times. Finally, the bird loosed the peculiar piece and a small white-colored item disappeared into the branches.

"Good for you, little one." Della smiled at its success. Expecting the bird to continue on in its flight, she was surprised to see it jump down into the branches, seemingly searching for the burden it had just released. "Let it go. Now you can fly unfettered."

But the bird was persistent. It found the white thing and used its beak to nudge the piece down through the branches. It fell to the ground directly in front of Della. The pigeon cooed and flew away.

Without opening it, Della accepted the gift with a small shout of, "Thanks." She stooped to pick it up. As Della rubbed the white piece, it began to unravel. It was the oddest thing. It was actually a piece of foolscap. It felt warm. Comfortable. Familiar. Exhilarating. That was ridiculous. It was just paper.

As she uncurled the missive, she read the curious words *send love.*

Something swelled within her. Her feet felt rooted, like the tree she stood under, but her arms wanted to take flight, like the pigeon she had befriended. It was the strangest sensation to read the words and feel an instant connection. To something and someone nameless. Faceless. It was almost as if the words were burned like an emblem onto her heart. Who wanted love? What kind of love were they in need of? Why did they need it now? What could she do about it? If anything.

The questions clanged through her mind, but she didn't have any time to reflect on them.

"Della, dear, you really must clean up before the party begins. I hope you don't mind me saying so. But, well, your dress, dear." Mavis waved her hand in the general direction of her frock. Della looked down but couldn't see any dirt. There must be something there though, otherwise Mavis wouldn't have pointed it out. Perhaps she had sweat too much. What an embarrassing thought.

Mavis had her hands clasped in front of her. There was no judgment in the suggestion to clean up, only a maternal figure manifesting her motherly nature. Della didn't stand on ceremony with the Ashbourne's. Despite being an earl's daughter, in Snowick Abbey she was just Della. And she preferred it that way.

So it was with only a mild amount of shock that Della received the next suggestion.

"Go freshen up in Colin's room." She must have had some amount of surprise registered on her face. "Oh don't be missish. The rest of the rooms are being readied for the houseguests. Quite a few people are remaining for the house party." Mavis waved her hand in the air. "Colin's not here, my dear. He won't be here until just before the garden party starts." She shooed her away. "Go on now." She pretended to hold her nose. "I've had a bath drawn for you as well. There's still plenty of time before any guests start to arrive."

"I really mustn't. It isn't prop–"

"My dear. Don't be silly. You'll be surrounded by people including a lady's maids. There is nothing improper in it at all. You're family." Mavis put her arm around Della and gently pushed her toward the house.

It made sense. Sort of. And really, there was an undying part of her that desperately wanted to go to Colin's room. Even if it was only for the purposes of cleaning up and taking a bath. A shiver ran through her. She would be naked in Colin's room. It was a delectably tempting thought.

Besides, Mavis was insisting. In fact, she was practically pushing Della into her son's room. It was fine. It was going to be perfectly fine.

It was going to be a series of mismanaging choices.

Chapter 3

THE MOMENT DELLA STEPPED across the threshold to enter Colin's room, she was in for trouble. The air in the room was charged. She was in his bedroom. Where he slept. Possibly naked. Just thinking about it made her want to slip out of her clothes and slide into his bed. Where he slept. Most likely naked. She wanted to roll around in his sheets. Where he slept. Definitely naked.

Della pressed her palms to her temples. She had to get ahold of herself. But the room even smelled like him. Of course it did. Bergamot and pine wafted through the air. It was so strong it was as if he had just been there.

That was silly of course, since Mavis had reassured her that Colin was not at home. And he wouldn't be home until later.

A lady's maid entered the room. "May I prepare you for your bath?"

Under every other circumstance, Della would have said yes, without a second thought. But she was in Colin's room. And she could have it all to herself. Why not engage in her fantasy? She would never have a second chance at this.

"I'll be alright. You need not return until I ring for you."

The maid curtsied and left the room.

Della hardly gave her space as she followed to the door and locked it.

Spinning back to face the room, she studied the space. It was masculine. Understated. Minimal decor. Soft tones. Just like Colin.

The bath water was steaming. She should soak now before it cooled off. She wouldn't snoop around and look through his things. That would be...well, just one look at his wardrobe wouldn't hurt.

She opened the door. She couldn't possibly touch...well, just one item.

Hastily, she pulled out one of his shirts and lifted it to her face. The smell was divine.

She would not pine for him and his pine scent. The second she left his bedroom, all of this was over.

Placing the note on his desk, she dropped her clothes faster than she had ever disrobed, and she slipped into his shirt. This was reckless. Scandalous. Absolutely not what she would ever do, under any other circumstance. Alas, it was too tempting not to give in this one time.

A yearning tore through her body and settled between her thighs. Hot. Pooling desire. She wanted to touch herself. Imagine it was him. Looking over at the bed, she wondered if she had enough time to pleasure herself. Her palm eased its way down to her mons, covered by his long shirt. Easing a little bit of pressure, she moaned. How she wanted to. Her body was on fire. At this internal temperature, if she settled into the bath, surely the steaming water would actually cool he r down.

Her body was aching. She walked over to the bed and rested her hand on one of the posters. Sliding a finger under the shirt and in between her folds, she moaned. Colin. Naked in his bed. That was all she was thinking when she grabbed her breast and massaged it. Her lower hand pressed in on her nub. Clothesless Colin. Broad shoulders. Thick thighs. Strong hands. Gentle lips.

The heat was pulsing through her body. Her legs bent slightly under the invisibly building weight. She rubbed faster. Felt herself opening, swelling.

"Uhh..." she moaned louder than she expected. Release.

Release so satisfying she didn't hear the click in the door.

***

If Colin could have imagined a thousand sights to see upon entering his bedroom, he would never have envisioned the splendor before him. Head rested on one of the posts of his bed, where he slept naked, would have been enticing enough. But the vixen was clad in his shirt. Long slender legs fully exposed for him to adore. He would know that bottom anywhere. And by God, how luscious it looked with only his shirt to cover it.

His cock hardened at the sight. The woman of his dreams was in his room.

"What are you doing here?" How he managed to utter that with a solid voice, he had no idea.

She whipped around, one arm over her breasts, one hand covering the patch he could see behind his shirt. Her face was flushed. She looked like a woman well bed.

Even her breathing was heavy. Which, now that he thought about it, so was his.

"Colin? What are you doing here?"

"This is my bedroom." He lifted his key as proof. Then, as if the key reminded him of the scandalous situation they were in, he flicked the lock on the door.

Somehow the key weighed pounds, so he walked over to his desk and laid it down right next to his note.

What the deuce was his note now doing in his room? This made no sense. Had Della found the note? Obviously it had fallen somewhere, since the pigeon returned noteless. But Della? What was fate trying to tell him? He already knew how she felt about him. What a cruel trick fate was playing.

Scowling, he lifted the note off the desk.

"What's this?"

Della scrambled over to him. She was so close that the fabric of her shirt–*his* shirt–brushed against him. He could reach out, grab her hip, and pull her in for a kiss. But he couldn't. She thought of him as a friend. He wanted a wife to love him. The same way his parents had loved each other. It spoiled him to have his parents' example of marriage, since he could settle for nothing less than love.

"It's a note." She grabbed it out of his hand. Her palm circling his fingers as she did so. They were friends. They had touched before. But never like this. With her wearing his shirt. Flushed. And so hot. He could feel the heat emanating from her body. He wanted to throw his body into her flames.

But he needed to focus. Why did she have his note?

"I can see that. What's it about? And why are you here?"

Seemingly picking the lesser of two evils, Della answered his first question only. "I don't know what it's about." She leaned closer, her shoulder pressed into his chest. "It just says, 'Send Love.' I don't know what it means, but I think someone has sent a message out to the universe."

Did she know it was his message? Was she playing coy? He studied her sky blue eyes. The same blue he had sent the pigeon loose into. He was lost in her depth. Her sincerity. There was no possibility of her faking anything.

Those deep blue eyes were staring into him. Still a touch glossy. And was that...fire? He shook his head. Impossible.

"What are you going to do about it?"

"I'm going to send a message back."

Colin stiffened. It was a reaction of self preservation to both the million questions swarming his head like bees as well as to her soft shoulder still pressed into his chest. "How?" he choked out.

Della withdrew her shoulder. Turning around, she leaned her bottom against the desk, legs outward. Did she forget what she was wearing? He could see everything now. Her arms weren't covering her in any way. He shouldn't peek at her nipples, but by God, they were right there. How was he to avoid them? They were practically poking him. His eyes darted down. God they were pert. Jutting out to him in greeting. He wanted to talk to them, but he threw a hand over his eyes and scrubbed his face.

"Colin? Are you alright?"

He groaned. He should take a step back, away from her. But if he did that then her full figure would be in view. Best to keep her close.

"Erm...yes. I'm fine. Just dandy."

A warm hand slid up his forearm. Too shocked to move, he watched from the corner of his eye as her hand went up, up, up, and rested on his shoulder. It wasn't abnormal for her to touch him. Except she was in his shirt, half naked. Fully naked underneath.

"You could help me." She patted his shoulder a couple of times. Just like a friend would do. That helped ease some tension in his lower parts.

"Sure. Anything." He muttered.

"Wonderful." Della turned around and practically shoved her bottom up against his cock as she bent over his desk to open a desk. "There must be some foolscap–ah, yes. Here's some." She readied the paper and quill. "Now, what shall we say?"

Maybe it was the proximity. She was so close he was basically breathing her in. Maybe it was her bum swaying slightly, brushing his cock. How did she not notice? He was so hard, he thought he was going to explode. Being a virgin, he didn't trust himself not to drench his breeches any second now. Yet another reason not to back away. He didn't want her to see how his body was reacting to her. Maybe he was yielding to fate and accepting its proffered token.

Whatever it was, Colin couldn't stop himself even if he wanted to. He blurted out the two words that would seal his fate.

"It's me."

Chapter 4

"THAT'S PERFECT!" DELLA LIFTED the quill to write. "Wait. That doesn't make sense. Perhaps I should write, 'I'm here. Come find me.' Like it's a game." She smiled to herself thinking of what fun she would love to have with her future husband.

"It's not a game."

She turned around again. It was dangerous either way, facing him or not. When she faced him, she wanted to reach out and touch his face. Run his fingers along his jaw, down his nose, trace his lips. But if she turned around, her body was being pulled back into him. She wanted to push her bottom against him and rub herself all over him. Ack! It was not enough to pleasure herself thinking about him. She wanted the real him for herself. At least once. In some small way even.

"Let's make it a game. It'll be so much more fun. I should love to marry a man who still loves to play." The fire in his eyes rattled her. Maybe she shouldn't have jumped to the conclusion that the sender of the message was looking for marriage. Or maybe she should have just kept her mouth shut about the note entirely. After all, it was none of his business.

"Fine. Sounds fun." But his tone sounded anything but fun. "Let's just write it and get this over with."

"You're no fun." She swatted his chest. His sculpted chest. The swat lasted perhaps longer than a normal swat might. Did he just flex?

"Write the note, Della."

"Fine." She returned to the equally dangerous position and scribbled the note. Waved it in the air a few times and let it flutter back to the desk. "Now where shall we put it? I don't want it to be too obvious? Oh! I've got it. I'll attach it to the collar of one of the pets up for adoption. Whoever finds the note will be the one that fate is handing me. That is the perfect test of fate. Don't you agree?"

By this time, Della was facing Colin again. His eyes were locked on her lips tightly enough to be reading them, yet he didn't respond. "Don't you think that's a good idea?"

"Yes. It's wonderful."

He looked entranced, staring at her lips in the same way she had stared at his. Did he want to kiss her? It couldn't be. If he had wanted to make a move, he would have done so at some point in the last couple of decades. Was he jealous that she was putting herself out there for another man to claim? The thought put a fire in her chest.

She was willing to make plenty of moves to secure the right husband, someone who loved her. So willing in fact, that she knew she was about to do something utterly reckless. She knew she was going to kiss him. But even if she kissed him, she wouldn't be the first to state her feelings. If he liked her, he would have to be the first. He could be shy as much as he wanted, but she had her pride as well. She wanted to know she was worth the effort. Worth stepping out of his comfort zone for. Lord knew the man was capable of trying new things. Surely he could try opening his mouth to simply say, *I like you*. She didn't even need to hear the love word first. As long as he verbalized his interest, she could keep the momentum going.

But those were thoughts for the future. Possibly a future that would never exist. And right now, she wanted to kiss him.

"Colin?" She slipped one hand up his shoulder, suddenly feeling dwarfed by his size.

"Yes?"

"Do you think you could help me with one more thing?" She slid her other hand up his shoulder.

"Mmm?"

"You know what will happen when the right man finds my note, don't you?" It was bold. Too bold. But she went for it. Her fingers entwined themselves in his hair. "He'll want to kiss me." A small huff rumbled through his throat. Interrupting whatever he was going to say, she pushed her hand further up into his hair. She watched with triumph as his eyes closed heavily. She leaned in, pushing her breasts against the solid wall of pure man before her. "I've never been kissed. I don't want to disappoint him." Closer, she rose up on tip toes, dragging her nipples up the wall, sending a shiver down her spine. "Can you just show me how it's done?"

She nudged him with her nose. She was going to get her kiss with the man she loved. And after that, if he still didn't make a move, she would give him up forever. Hopefully fate had the right man planned for her.

"Anything, Della. For you, anything."

His lips touched the corner of her mouth, and a gasp escaped her. He was so tender. Soft. Yet he was all man. But then he pulled away.

That couldn't be all. She hadn't come this far, risked this much, for only that.

"Please Colin. Show me. As a friend."

***

AS A FRIEND. THE words seared through him. His hands gripped her hips, locked in place. Blood rushed to his ears. The pounding in his head matched a hammering in his heart. So yes, he would show her. As a friend. He would kiss her just like a friend might. He could refrain from any passion. He would just keep his mouth s hut.

He leaned in to brush his lips against hers again. And then he was going to pull away. Easy. But that sigh. How could one sigh push the boundaries of propriety so much? He dipped his head again, but this time he was met with her slightly parted lips. From the sigh, he supposed. But it didn't matter, sigh or not, he matched her lips.

Her hands were gripping him harder. Pushing further up into his hair. She was raising her body again, rubbing those pointed nipples against his chest. Again. God, he wanted her. He tilted her head, the kiss deepened, he met her tongue with his. Lapping at her mouth. Sucking on her. And then another groan. Her sounds were arousing him. His cock fully tented his breeches. He could just lift her up on this desk and thrust into her. She was the only woman he had ever imagined making love to. And here he was, as her friend, teaching her how to kiss. Did she know the limits she was pushing him to?

She moaned inaudible words. And he had to. He just had to. He lifted her onto the desk and stepped between her legs.

Hands roamed under her shirt. Her cunny was naked and exposed, on his desk. It was probably dripping wet, leaving him a message he would never forget. Never erase.

He couldn't bring himself to say her name. It was too intimate. It was for lovers to share in passion, not friends in practice.

Her hands cinched around his waist and pulled him closer. She was on the edge of the desk, arching herself into him. Rubbing herself against him, fully aware of her body and what would bring her pleasure.

"You know what you want." He whispered hoarsely in her ear. He wanted her to say, *You. I want you.*

"Yes." She moaned as she pushed herself harder against his cock. "But I've only had...my hand before."

The knowledge that she knew pleasure and gave it to herself caused a tightening in his sack. "Then use me now. Take it."

He bit down on her neck. Not wanting to leave a visible mark, he licked down to her nipple and tugged it into his mouth through his shirt. He would never wash this shirt again. Her groan filled his ears, and if he would let it, his heart and soul. Though he was a virgin, he had still been with a few women and had learned how to please them. He just never inserted his cock into someone. Here and now, it was everything in him not to ram himself into her dripping cunny. With his thumb, he found her nub, swollen, pulsing. Gently, he feathered a to uch.

Her shout poured into him. He couldn't stop it–no matter how hard he tried–from infiltrating his soul. And he had only one response, he released into his breeches. Muffling his groan in her smooth neck.

Both of their breaths were coming in hard and fast.

"Was that enough practice?" He had to ask.

If he could have predicted the answer, he never would have asked.

"Yes." She heaved a deep breath. "You're a good friend, Colin. A very good friend. Perhaps the best."

Chapter 5

"JUST FRIENDS THEN?" THE deep voice rumbled. Della could feel the rapid movements of Coline's chest more than she could see them.

Why was he asking her that? If he wanted more, then he should just say it. Hadn't she already made enough first moves? The erratic beating of her heart was not slowing. It was a confused mixture of passion and growing vexation.

But there was to be no time to finish the conversation, for the rap on the door interrupted them.

RAP. RAP. RAP.

"Della, my dear? Are you still in there? It's time to get things started?"

"It's your mother," Della hissed.

"Hide." Colin urged.

"Me? You hide."

"It's my room."

"Didn't you hear her? She's looking for me." Della watched as a strange look flashed across Colin's face. Disbelief. Confusion. She didn't have time to explain the peculiar situation. "Just hide." She pushed herself off of the desk and slammed into his chest. His hands steadied her. When she looked up, she melted into him. She wanted to stay here. Answer his question. Really, she wanted to force him to answer his own question.

A second set of knocks came.

"Della?"

"I'm here. Just one moment."

Della pushed a bewildered Colin backward toward his wardrobe. He slipped in while she went to answer the door.

Opening it a crack, she managed to control her voice. "Your Grace, I'll be out in a thrice."

Mavis' eyes scanned her face, and tried to peek into the room. "Are you alright? Don't you need help getting dressed?"

"I'll be fine, thank you."

"I had a dress sent to the room. Did you see it?"

In fact, Della hadn't seen it, so she took a second to turn around and look about the room. There it was, draped over a chair.

"Ah yes. Thank you. I shall be fine. See you soon." And then Della did the most ungracious thing she had ever done. She closed the door before Mavis could get in another word.

But it didn't work. Mavis called out, "I'll just wait here for you, my dear. I have a most urgent matter to discuss with you. Hurry up now."

Closing and locking the door, she slumped against its hard frame. It was nothing compared to resting against Colin's frame.

Colin. In the wardrobe. What was she going to do about him?

He stepped out and into the room, looking as handsome as ever. His gray eyes and wet sand colored hair. Those waves. She had snaked her fingers through those locks. Gripped them. Twisted them. A dream come true. And now...now was the aftermath. A castle made of sand washed away by the waves. He didn't declare himself. He didn't say anything. But that was his default mode. How could she fault him? She knew how he felt and had known for a long time. She brushed her hands down the shirt she was wearing, wondering if there was any way she could keep it. Hide it under her dress somehow. It was absolute foolishness. She had to let go of him. Him and his soft as silk shirt.

"You have to help me dress." She pointed at the dress she was about to don. It looked forlorn. Probably a silly thought to think about a dress. As she thought about putting on the new dress, it felt symbolic. Like somehow she was donning a new woman. A woman stepping into her future. And that future was not likely to be the one she had always hoped for. Instead, she was about to clad herself with a hope and a prayer. And a silly little note, that only the hands of fate could control. Should anyone other than the right man–whoever that was now–find the note, she would just play it off as a joke. Della shook the errant thoughts from her mind. "Help me dress. Please. Your mother is waiting outside the door."

Without a word he walked to where she pointed, and she met him there. In front of the fire, he stood waiting for her to lift her shirt. She should have told him to close his eyes. She should have stepped into the dress first and been modest about the whole affair.

Modest? She had just come all over his breeches. And she knew he had come too. She had seen the mark through his falls. Modesty was out the window. Give the poor sap one more look at what he was missing. She turned her back to him and stepped into the dress. He was directly behind her. She pulled his shirt over her head.

She expected a gasp. A sound of appreciation of any kind. Nothing came. Except...the lightest touch of his index finger. It touched the base of her neck and then gradually dragged down her spine, stopping right at the top of her cleft. Like a pin, he held it in place.

All of her life, she felt as though she had understood Colin. He was kind-hearted, gentle, selfless. He took care of people and animals. If someone needed something, anything, they knew they could ask Colin. For a favor. For a ride. For an extra ticket. For the last biscuit. Well, that last one wasn't entirely true. He had a sweet tooth. So while he might give you the last sandwich or glass of wine, he would probabl y finish off a treat if it were already in his hand. Yes, he'd give you the shirt off of his own back, but not the dessert in his hand. Oh yes, she knew Colin only all too well. But at this moment, she couldn't read what was going through his mind.

"Let's get you dressed," he finally said in a gruff voice. And then the pin was lifted. He squatted down to lift the dress. With each button, his fingers brushed her skin.

It took all of her willpower to resist the shivers eager to race up and down her spine.

When he was done, he braced his hands on her shoulders. "All done."

She turned her jaw toward one of his hands, a whisper eked out. "Thank you." She felt his body swaying into hers, from the corner of her eyes could see his head leaning in. But she didn't want another kiss. She wanted his words. A declaration of any kind.

She stepped away from the warmth. The familiarity. Her friend. "I'll see you at the party."

Chapter 6

IT WAS A THREEWAY battle between will, dignity, and impulsiveness. Dignity won. Though it didn't feel like much of a win as Della left the bedroom. If she had voiced her interest in him, would he have reciprocated? And even if he had, would she ever feel like a woman chased? Would she ever feel chosen? Maybe it was silly girlish dreams. Maybe tomorrow she would wake up and change her mind, walk over to his house, and pour out her heart. But for now, she resolved to stay strong. Hold out for him to make a move.

"You had better make the first move, my dear." Mavis wiggled her arm through Della's.

Had she been speaking aloud? To Colin's mother?

Not prone to stuttering except in the event her unrequited lover's mothers could read her thoughts, Della intelligibly uttered, "Uh–u mm–when..I mean, what do you mean, Your Grace?"

"Come now. We both know what's going on. So are you going to tell him or not?"

"I don't think so." She shook her head. It did not shake loose the confusion.

"Don't you think it's about time you told him?"

"I think he should say something first. He's the man."

"Oh my dear. Since you're showing your youth. I shall show my age. Men don't know what women think. They hardly know what they think."

She knew. Everything? Had she planned the scandalous encounter in the bedroom? She couldn't have. Could she? "In that case...um...perhaps I should tell him how I feel."

"Well, of course he would love to know." Mavis patted her arm and peered into her eyes with a knowing look. Then she pursed her lips, a trait Colin had probably learned from her, and gazed down the hallway. "That would be wise. It would move things along quite nicely. As he wants everyone to adopt a pet, he would be overjoyed to know that you are finally going to get one. Aside from your fish of course."

Right. Of course, that's what they were talking about. The garden party in which everyone would be adopting a pet. That made significantly more sense than Mavis knowing her feelings toward her son and plotting a scandalous tryst for said son.

"Yes. I shall tell him the first chance I get."

"Good plan, my dear." She patted her hand. "The guests are arriving. Colin should be here soon. We shall have tea and then bid for the darling animals Colin has rescued."

"Wonderful." How exceedingly wonderful.

The garden party underway, Della was not exactly avoiding Colin, but she wasn't exactly not avoiding him either.

It was busy playing hostess. It was even busier when said hostess was seeing to every possible whim of every attending guest, save the charming sponsor of the event. Even her cousin Rose, one of the many guests, was wondering why Della was so tense. That was a conversation to avoid at all costs. Never wanting to marry, Rose would not understand the predicament Della currently found herself in. So Della flitted between guests, avoiding any semblance of serious conversation, until she could flit no more.

Considering how much effort she had put into flittering, it was high time for Della to grab a snack. It was often that way in events, she hardly ate or drank a thing, caring for everyone else to be having a good time.

Making her way to the dessert table, she looked for her favorite treat. The one she had insisted be part of the event. Apple custard pie. She could already taste the sweet apples. But as she arrived at the table, she noticed they were all gone. Her shoulders slumped for a moment before she regained her composure. It was just a treat.

A throat cleared. Then cleared again. "Ahem," came the third, and successful, attempt to gain her attention.

"Oh, it's you." She glanced at Colin and quickly looked away. How could she make a good excuse not to talk to him in this exact moment? But wait, what was that in his hand?

"Looking for one of these?" He wiggled his spoon in the air. "I snagged the last apple custard pie. The first one was delicious. The second one was divine. I think this third one will be–"

"What do you want for it?" It was a long shot. He rarely gave up his treats. But he had already had two. Surely he wouldn't ask for much.

The long perusing look he took of her from toe to top alluded otherwise.

"Now that you mention it...I could think of a couple of things."

"Colin, please." She moved closer to him, if only to shut him up. And possibly grab the treat. That would never happen.

He chuckled. "Tell me which animal the note is on."

Her eyebrows crinkled. "Why would you ask that when you know what's at stake?"

"Perhaps that's why—"

A loud voice boomed across the garden. "It's time to start the auction. All of these pets need a home, and all the funds raised will go back into The Animal Safety and Rescue Society. Please take your places."

Colin nudged her with his elbow. Sparks flew through her arm digging into her heart.

"Are you going to tell me?" He flashed a small and waved the dessert under her nose.

She could easily have told him it was tucked in with the hedgehog. She could twist fate's arm and make it all work out for herself. But if she was doing that, why not just tell Colin her feelings and see how he reacted? No. She steeled herself to follow through with one plan at a time. If this one didn't work, she could try a new one later.

"No."

"No? Really, come on Dells."

Just changing that one letter off her name increased the intimacy she felt with him. He had often called her *Dells,* and very few people did. She could count on one hand those familiar enough with her to use the moniker.

"No. I shan't play with fate that way." She moved closer to auction. "Let's take our places."

"Here." He offered the apple custard pie to her.

Oh, he had to be sweet on top of everything else, didn't he? She took the pie, making sure not to pay any mind to the burn felt along her fingers in the exchange. "That's very generous of you considering you already had two."

That chuckle again. She loved to hear his laughter. "I didn't have two. I was just trying to make you jealous. That was going to be my first. It's all yours though."

Well...she was speechless. Thoughtless, even.

"First up we have..."

The auctioneer trailed on announcing first a dog, then a cat, and third a canary. Possibly one from the mines. Della was too lost in thought, or was it thoughtlessness, to notice anything. Until he called the hedgehog. It was the last pet of the party up for adoption. Where Colin had rescued a hedgehog, she had no clue. Upon seeing the cute little thing, her body stiffened. This was the moment where fate would play its cards.

"How much for the hedgehog?"

"Two pounds," Colin called out. He was bidding. Did he know?

She shot him a look. He met her eyes with the calmest, surest gray she had ever seen. The soft kind of gray that was dead center between black and white. Not undecided, but decidedly center. The thoughts made little sense except that she knew he knew about the hedgehog. And if he knew that her note was in the hedgehog, and he knew what she hoped to be the outcome–marriage–then... then what was he doing?

"Colin," she hissed. "That's the one."

"Three pounds," came a shout from the crowd.

"Who was that?" Colin looked back. "What the bloody hell is Evan doing?"

"I thought that was Felix?" Della looked between the twin brothers, one on either side of Mavis. Odd, that. Mavis was staring straight at her with a coy look on her lips.

Colin whirled back around. "Four pounds."

Not missing a beat, "Five pounds."

"Six."

"Seven."

"Is this a magical hedgehog," the auctioneer began. But the brothers were heated now.

"Eight."

"Twelve."

"Fifty."

"One hundred." Evan called out.

Gasps were heard all over. The lady beside Colin swooned. Just in time, Colin caught her in his arms to protect her from falling.

"Sold to Lord Evan."

"Wait, one hundred and–"

The claps drowned out Colin's last attempt at a bid.

Della eyes raced back and forth between Evan and Colin. Colin was her choice. And seemingly she was his too? But Evan would get the hedgehog and the note. What game was fate playing? Why had she entrusted her future to fate? She could just take it back. She didn't have to follow through on her plans. They were all silly plans to begin with anyway.

Evan sauntered over.

"Nice try, Colin. But this one's mine." The look he gave Della sent shivers up her spine. And not the good kind. True, Evan was a delight. But not for her.

"Stick to your homing pigeons, brother. I'm sure you'll figure out the messaging system soon enough."

Della shook her head. Pigeons? Messages? She glared at Colin. He was the original sender.

He had known all along.

Chapter 7

WELL, THAT WAS NOT a good look. Della had fire in her eyes. And not the kind he had witnessed earlier in the bedroom.

Bosh! How was he going to dig himself out of this one? Why hadn't he just told her how he felt? Why hadn't he confessed to writing the note in the first place? He had tried. Those two itsy bitsy words had felt enormous in the moment. He *had* said, *It's me*. She had just misunderstood him. And maybe that was fate playing with them both. Either way, it was all a huge mess now. It could have been avoided if he had been honest. If he had been courageous enough to accept her rejection earlier. Now everything was that much harder. That much more complicated. They had been together. Not fully. But as fully as he had ever been with a woman. More so. She was the only one that made him feel himself. There was no way in his lifetime that he was going to let Evan get that note.

All eyes were on him. Now was his chance. He needed to shake fate up a bit. He raced over to the auctioneer and grabbed the hedgehog. Carefully. "Where's the note?" He asked the auctioneer.

"What note?"

"This little hedgehog came with a rolled up piece of paper, did he not?" He was about to feel all kinds of embarrassment if he had misread Della's body language upon seeing the hedgehog up for bid.

"You mean this little thing? I didn't realize it was part of the–"

"Give me that." He whipped it out of the man's hands. "Please." Returning the hedgehog to the auctioneer, he added, "And I'll be back for her."

Then he raced over to Della. "I've got it. I found it. I'm the one."

He didn't mean to say it loudly. He hated public speeches. It was why he never spoke at the garden parties, despite being the sponsor. Some people of the *ton* thought him rude, but most chalked it up to being an eccentricity. Yet here he was, waving the flimsy piece of rolled up foolscap in the air, shouting.

"It's me, Della. I found it."

He could see the hurt in her eyes, and his heart withered. "Don't be mad at me. I'm an idiot. A bacon-brained fool. But I couldn't let you go. Not after..." he looked back at the house, "that. And not to him." He pointed to his brother.

"Hey!"

"Another time, Evan." Mavis patted her other son on the arm, and Colin was sure he heard her whisper to Evan, "You did good."

"Dells, please, hear me out." And he knew everyone could hear. But he didn't care. "Let the whole world hear, as long as you hear and know the truth. I was foolish for thinking I had time to tell you. And then a bigger fool for being too afraid to tell you. I thought you only wanted to be my friend, and if that's all you can give, I will gladly accept it. I love you. I've always loved you. I want to marry you. Spend my life with you. Being your friend. Your very good friend. Perhaps even your best friend. Della, will you marry me?"

There was a pause. Too long if anyone asked his opinion. No one did. But then there was a grin. And it almost made up for the pause.

"As long as you promise to give me your apple pie custard should I ever ask for it."

"We shall have apple pie custard every day."

"Then yes. My answer is yes."

And the smile that lit her face shot through him. He swept her up into his arms and swung her around. And then, since a public speech was not enough, he kissed her on the lips in front of everyone.

When he put her down, he overheard his mother saying the strangest thing.

"It's about time," Mavis whispered. "I couldn't push it much further than I did."

***

The garden party was a success. All the pets had been adopted. A large amount of money had been raised. And Colin was feeling pretty hopeful about working with his homing pigeons in the near future.

For the present future, he was staring at Della, as they stood alone in her guest bedroom. Everyone had gone to sleep already, and he had snuck into her room. It was only fair.

"I needed to see you again, Dells."

"Do you think this is proper, Colin?" She was teasing, and he loved it. "I'm not sure my body can handle three times in one day."

Three? So she had been up to something before he arrived. God, how that made his cock swell within his breeches.

"I'll be gentle." His arms weaved around her waist. "And we don't have to do...all of it. I just want to feel you in my arms again, knowing you're mine now."

"I see. Well, I think we should. Do all of it, that is."

Resting his head against her forehead, he sighed. "I'm so happy to hear you say that. You know you're a vixen, don't you? The way you have captured my heart, it could be done by no one else. But I didn't want to go into marriage a virgin, so I'm very happy to hear you say you want more. I know I shall have to marry you quickly, as I can't stand to be apart from you for long. I don't want to cause a scandal, you know?"

"More than the one you did earlier today? You know there will be talk in the *ton* of your grand speech, And the kiss of course."

"Let them talk. As long as I'm kissing you, they can say whatever they want."

"Mmm...I like the way you think." She kissed his neck. "I didn't know you were a virgin, Colin."

"Does it bother you?"

"Of course not. I think we shall discover each other together. I'm excited. And...well, I feel special."

"You are special. You are the only one for me."

"I love you, Colin. I've always loved you. I was just waiting for you."

His heart soared at the words. "Now you have me. It seems we have both been waiting for each other. No more waiting."

He nibbled on her neck. His heart was racing. His legs already feeling weak, he moved them toward the bed. He tucked loose tresses behind her ear, then grazed her dress. "May I?"

"Yes."

He pushed the dress off her shoulder and pressed kisses to the exposed skin. Creamy, soft skin that he could kiss for days. Hands were swarming the dress, undoing buttons. Clamoring to get her out of the restrictive clothing.

"Dells, I went feral when I saw you in my shirt earlier, but now I want to see all of you." Hands continued to work, both on him and her. The layers were strewn on the floor, and she stood before him, a shining shimmering light. Him still in his breeches, but shirtless, he held his breath when she removed her last article of clothing. "I want to take my time with you. All of you." His hands absorbed the tremors going through her body. Then those same hand stroked her sides and slowly reached down and palmed her mons. "Dells, I want to take my time with your quim. Taste her. Drink from you."

"Is that what lovers do?"

"Yes, some do. I would love you that way, if you let me."

He could see desire in her eyes, and curiosity. No shame. She nodded.

"Lay back, darling." She took out the pins from her hair, placing them on her nightstand, as she relaxed on the bed.

He could see her cunny, already glossy. All he wanted was to taste her. Know her. Love her. He placed a few kisses on her shoulder. The tops of her breasts. Her stomach. Her center. Gently, he pushed her legs open wider. Nibbled on her inner thigh. Her hands rushed into his hair, massaging his scalp. And then he had to know her taste.

He licked into her. Once. Twice. The gasp. Her hands. The pressure to continue. The moan. He licked again and again. Propelled by her sounds and rewarded by her taste. He hummed his pleasure, and her legs tightened around his ears.

"Mmmm...come for me, Dells. Pour out a drink and let me lap at your cup."

Her legs were locked in place and he lifted her hips gently, then sucked on her nub. The cry came from her mouth, but the tears came from her quim. He drank each one.

Once her legs relaxed, he looked up at her face. "God, you're delicious."

Through her panting, she asked, "What about you? I want to know how you taste."

His already steel-solid cock twitched in his breeches. "Yes, one day, darling. Tonight, he wants to see his new home."

"Yes, come home. Please Colin." Strewn on his bed, a goddess. His lover. His future wife. The only woman he would truly love and make love to. He was ready.

He stood and dropped his breeches and then kneeled on the bed in between her legs. Her quim was glistening. She was ready too.

"May I?"

"Don't wait another second, Colin."

He touched his tip to her entrance and groaned. This was what he had waited for. He drew a line down her nub and shivered. It was time. He slipped into her. An inch. Then another. She was drawing him in. He groaned. About to lose his balance, he placed a palm on either side of her. When she sucked him in fully, their groans met each other. How could he have been such a fool to wait so long for her? It didn't matter. She was his now. And he was hers.

Her arms wrapped around his neck, and they met in the air for a kiss. An insatiable kiss. A kiss that mimicked how his cock was sliding in and out of her. Teasing. As if he would ever leave her.

"God, you're so tight. So wet."

"You're so big, Colin."

He could feel her hard nipples rubbing against his chest. How could they be closer? How could he know her more than this? He had the rest of his life to find out. But thank God, somehow the next thrust brought them closer. His pelvic bone pushing into her nub. She clenched around his cock and squeezed him. His head fell back. His teeth clenched. A growl thundered out of him. He meant to pull out, but there was no time. He released into her. Her pulses continued, squeezing him again. And again. Squeezing him dry.

"God, Dells. You are my home. I can't wait to have you all to myself and start a family with you."

"Mmm... yes." Her arms lay limp at her sides. A smile danced softly across her face. "I can feel that."

He chuckled. "I might have to marry you tomorrow. I can't wait."

"No more waiting. I agree."

He rolled over and tucked her into his arms. "What are we going to do?"

"We're going to be happy, and we're going to be bold. We're going to live life together, the way we want to live it."

And that's exactly what he was asking.

Turn the page for more in The Ashbourne Legacy series.

The Rogue and the Rose: Chapter 1

1816 England

HER MIDDLE NAME WAS Danger. Actually. And it was *actually* the result of a ridiculous dare that her parents had lost many years ago. She had yet to hear the full story, but one day she would drag it out of them. Besides for the obvious reasons that is was a ludicrous name to give a baby girl, it was also ridiculous because she wasn't the least bit dangerous. Or so she thought, at least.

"You know what's going to happen when you get on that horse, don't you?" Hope taunted.

"What's that?" Emma knew she was in for an earful. Though she admired her best friend Hope, youngest sister to seven brothers in the Ashbourne clan, at this moment, Emma wasn't keen on hearing any input from anyone. It didn't matter how long she had known and loved Hope.

"The men here will never see you the same again."

"They haven't seen me in the first place. Besides, most of the men here are your brothers, so it really doesn't matter."

Hope chuckled. "There are plenty of men at this house party besides my brothers, but is there any one brother in particular you've been noticing?" Emma felt a small nudge in her ribs from a bony elbow.

She scoffed. "Not a single one. You know I don't want to get married." She had seen too many women who had relied on their husbands, only to be widowed and destitute. No, marriage was not an option for her. She would be self-sufficient. That way no one could disappoint her.

"Mmm...still thinking that way are we?"

"I don't know about you, but I know about me, and I am still thinking that way. I have no use for a stodgy old man who will only view me as his property."

"And what of the handsome ones?"

"Fate doles out looks or intelligence. Not both together."

Feigning injury, Hope placed a hand on her chest. "And how, pray tell, did we elude fate's miserly ways?"

"We again? Well, you most assuredly escaped. You are a rare specimen. But it took eight tries." Emma's grin broke her face, and it was contagious.

"Yes, well, you also escaped. And it only took a few tries." Hope was referring to Lady Emma's three older brothers, the oldest of which was Isaac, the Duke of Benhelm. Being the youngest girls, each in a family of all boys immediately sealed the bond between the two girls, and they had maintained their friendship over nearly twenty years. "But back to my original point, my bold, beautiful, *and* brilliant friend," Hope ignored the mock glare Emma threw her way. "If you get on that horse, you're sealing your fate. Men don't want to marry a woman that can beat them in a horse race."

A laugh burst out of Emma. "First of all, we both know my fate has already been sealed. I'm three-and-twenty with no suitors to speak of. I'm happy to take my place on the back of the shelf so I can move on with my own life plans. Which," she pointed to Hope, "you know you are sworn to secrecy on for the time being.

With pursed lips, Hope crossed her heart.

"Second of all, I'm tired of holding back. Finally, look around. It's just your brothers. There's no one here to even consider marrying. I really must get on the horse now, because as much as men don't want a woman who will beat them in a horse race, they would much less want one who will come in last place. And I'll not take the pity offers that would result from that outcome."

Hope shrugged her shoulders. "Well, I wish you luck! I shall see you back at the house. Perhaps I'll catch Dawson napping and finally trick him into telling me where he's been skulking out to at night."

Dawson. One of Hope's middle brothers. That was a man who truly deserved the name Danger. In fact, the scandal sheets were always warning the young debutants away from him. Not knowing what he did with himself when he disappeared for days and nights at a time, the *on dit* could only speculate the worst. Gambling. Brothels. Drunken binges. He was out all night. No wonder he napped every day. One wouldn't think to call a napper, Dangerous, but when said napper took to the streets all night, it was a different story. Dawson. Yes, he was the most dangerous of all of Hope's brothers, so Emma always steered clear of him.

The reverie cost her precious moments. When she regained focus in her eyes, remaining on the field was just Emma and a few men ready to race. Isaac and a handful of Hope's other brothers were the only ones in attendance for this private event of the house party. And their horses were getting restless.

Emma swung herself up on the horse just shy of the word, "Go!"

As luck would have it, her horse shied from the exclaimed *Go*, and it took a moment to get him under control. The other riders had taken off and were already out of sight rounding a bend. It was a longer race than normal, so she still had time to catch up. If only her horse would stop grazing.

She nudged the horse and soon he was lengthening his strides. Wind in her hair. Sun on her face. Power between her legs. A winning future ahead. Nothing could be better.

***

LORD DAWSON, FOURTH STRAPPING and dashing son in the Ashbourne family, was out for a leisurely ride. Carving out time for himself at least for a few hours in the day either to think about his new mining project or just to clear his mind was necessary. Especially during a house party when his attention was constantly demanded. And by women no less, despite his reputation. By beautiful woman, sure, but even that got old. How many more one-sided conversations did he have to endure this season? Even though he wasn't the duke in the family, not even close, he was wealthy enough to draw their attention. And somehow that meant that the women who sought him out made themselves biddable blank sheets. Not that they all *were* biddable blank sheets, that's just what they presented to him. No matter, he didn't want to marry anyway. As long as he could find pleasure between some of those sheets, he would be fine. And since widows were not in short supply, he was always fine. Innocents were off limits, of course. Especially one pert little future spinster always hanging around his sister. Emma. She was a challenge and a half. Sometimes he just needed to avoid her and the jolts of current that flooded him when he was around her. What a damn nuisance they were. He wasn't about to bring such an innocent into his dangerous life.

A yelp broke into his thoughts. He looked toward the sound, and there, of all people, was that pert little vexatious spinster. Only, she didn't look so pert. Her hands were in the air, the reins loose, and had that been a cry for help?

That horse was galloping at breakneck speed. A break-Emma's-neck speed.

Dash it! Dawson turned his horse to race after her.

The thundering hoofbeats of his horse were catching up to her. But her own horse's movements must have been too loud. She didn't even take a second to look back, or perhaps she was too afraid to move. He was right on her tail.

Then, the horses were right beside each other, but Dawson couldn't reach the reins. They had slipped out of sight. "Emma, take my hand. Hold on." Without a second warning, he wrapped his arm around her lower back and twister her over, around, and onto his horse.

Chest to chest, he was immediately enveloped by the scent of roses and encased by her thighs. Thighs that were on the verge of being exposed due to the way her skirts were piling around his groin. His groin was in a state of shock at the sight and feel of her legs wrapped around him. Something was surging through him. In one area in particular. Must be adrenaline. His heart was just racing from the speed they had been riding at. It had nothing to do with the arms clenched around his neck.

Distractedly, he slowed his horse to a trot.

“Are you alright? You–”

“What are you doing?”

They said simultaneously.

“I just rescued you from a runaway horse you had no control over. What do you think I’m doing?”

“Did it look like I needed saving?”

“Yes.”

“No.” They overlapped each other’s speech again, she answering her own–evidently hypothetical–question.

“Dawson, I was in the middle of a race.”

“Against who? Yourself?”

“Ugh. I could have won if you had just let me be.”

“I hate to break it to you, sweetheart, but whoever you were racing was miles ahead. You didn’t stand a chance with that horse.”

“You don’t know me.”

“Apparently you don’t know that horse.”

Stay Connected

Please leave me a review :)

If you like my books, please leave me a review. You can find my books through my Amazon Author page here.

https://amazon.com/author/elianapiers

Find me and follow me online:

1. My Facebook READER GROUP: Eliana Piers' Beau Monde Reader Group

2. My Facebook Page: www.facebook.com/elianapiers

3. Instagram: @ElianaPiersAuthor

4. Tiktok: @ElianaPiers

Browse My Bookstore

https://www.elianapiers.com
You'll find **bundled books** and **book boyfriend swag**.

Read The Good Dukes:

- Good Duke Gone Cold
    - http://www.books2read.com/GoodDukeGoneCold
- Good Duke Gone Hard
    - http://www.books2read.com/GoodDukeGoneHard
- Good Duke Gone Bad
    - http://www.books2read.com/GoodDukeGoneBad
- Good Duke Gone Low
    - http://www.books2read.com/GoodDukeGoneLow
- Good Duke Gone Far
    - http://www.books2read.com/GoodDukeGoneFar

Read the Dukes for Christmas Fairytale series:

- A Beauty for a Duke
    - www.books2read.com/ABeautyForADuke
- An Ember for a Duke
    - https://www.books2read.com/AnEmberForADuke
- A Slumber for a Duke
    - https://www.books2read.com/ASlumberForADuke

Read the Ashbourne Legacy series:

- The Blighter and the Bluestocking
- The Scoundrel and the Scientist
- The Virgin and the Vixen

Thank You

Thanks Dad. Falconer… homing pigeons… same same

Thank you to my beta readers, Jenni Simonis and Jordan Lynch. xoxoxo

Thank you to all my ARCs. Thank you for loving my characters :D

Thank you to my loving husband. Yes. Another series ;)

Thank you to you, my *beau monde*! I love that you love my books.

Much love!

About the Author

Eliana Piers, award-winning and best-selling author, has been writing and singing stories since she was five years old. After feeling inspired by authors like Julia Quinn, Tessa Dare, and Minerva Spencer, Eliana decided to test her quill on the page.

Writing about love and how two people come to connect and share parts of their souls with each other is now an obsession.

It's not worth it if you don't laugh, learn, or love while you're in it.

Eliana lives in Canada where she drinks an ice cap every day.

Also By Eliana Piers

Side Stories

Sweeten the Rogue (Novelette)
The Rogue and the Reader (Novelette)

The Good Dukes Series

Good Duke Gone Cold
Good Duke Gone Hard
Good Duke Gone Bad
Good Duke Gone Low
Good Duke Gone Far
Coming soon (2024): Good Duke Gone Wild

Dukes for Christmas Fairytale series

A Beauty for a Duke
An Ember for a Duke
A Slumber for a Duke
MORE to COME in 2024!

The Ashbourne Legacy series

The Blighter and the Bluestocking
The Scoundrel and the Scientist
The Virgin and the Vixen
The Rogue and the Rose
The Rake and the Writer
The Wastrel and the Wallflower
The Spy and the Spinster

Read More: Dukes for Christmas

Turn the page for Chapter 1 of Book 1 in the Dukes for Christmas series: *A Beauty for a Duke.*

Beauty with brains meets a big, grumpy Beast just before Christmas. Only a third wheel and a long carriage ride are in their way...

A Beauty for a Duke

Chapter 1

1816, England

JUST ONE MORE CHAPTER. She had to finish just one more chapter. It could easily be done before–

"Sofie," drawled her curvy, and heavy-bosomed friend, Fia. Since childhood the two had been inseparable. What more did they need than for their names to complete each other? Sofie and Fia together since six. Or was it five? It was all the same. They had so many shared memories together that if one forgot, the other was likely to remember. Though, if the truth were being told, and it usually was among the two of them, Fia was the one with the better memory for events. And Sofie was more dependable for remembering ideas. And making plans. Or, more accurately, roping the two of them into haphazardly constructed plans.

Which was exactly how the two had met. It was Sofie's first time going out alone to buy bread for the day. Her father had finally allowed her that small amount of freedom, so she skipped all the way there. When she looked up into the eyes of a small girl about her size, she said, "I must have lost my coins skipping all the way here. Oh no! Papa will never trust me with money again."

The little girl behind the counter replied, "I'll help you find them. That's what friends are for. Papa won't mind, will you Papa?" She swiveled her bouncing crimson curls to her father, the baker, who was already nodding his head.

She darted out from behind the counter saying, "I'm Fia by the way."

"I'm Sofie."

Fia squealed, "Oh, that's perfect! I always wanted my name to be Sofie, and now, together, we shall make the best of friends with the loveliest of names."

Sofie grinned, "We're friends?"

"Why not?"

She couldn't agree more.

"Let's go." And the two girls had pranced off in search of treasure. Not only had they found the coins, but they had also swam with mermaids and fought dragons the entire way. Much to their surprise, they both returned home without a scratch. From that day on, not a day had passed without the two of them seeing each other. They knew all there was to know about the other.

So that's why Fia could easily read Sofie's mind as she stared at the book in front of her.

"I know you are probably convincing yourself that you can squeeze in one more chapter of reading, but really, I can't serve the entire tavern by myself."

Sofie was leaning over her open book, head down, breasts resting on the high table in the backroom of The Crowned Rose, owned by her father, Richard. She tucked a stray chestnut strand behind her ear.

Finally she glanced up to find Fia sliding her hand over her perfectly coiffed crimson hair and then flicking an invisible fleck from her bodice. How she always managed to look so put together and kept up, Sofie couldn't be sure. Sofie was never unkempt, or...unput together, but she could certainly use a few extra pins at any given time.

"Alright, Fia, I'm coming. Just one more page."

The eye that her friend gave her spoke almost as loudly as the din coming from the main room just beyond the door. It must be a full house. *When had that happened?* Last she checked, which could have been hours ago, half of the tables were open. She had even thought to attempt some Christmas decorating after she finished her chapter. Or entire book. Whichever came first.

"Alright, alright. Just let me finish this sentence."

"I'll wait." Fia tapped her foot.

"Done," Sofie placed her paper rose bookmark in between the pages and pushed the book into the large pocket in her frock. To be sure Sofie didn't pull a fast one, Fia threaded her arm through Sofie's, and coaxed her back to work.

Sofie entered the chaos, grateful for the work she had. Being in Derbyshire near the Duke of Somersby's estate, despite its small size, the public house had the pleasure of serving many a patron from England and beyond.

Perhaps not now that Christmas was fast-approaching. Everyone would be tucked away in their warm homes, sidling up to fires and roasting treats. If not now, then at least within the next week. Which meant that within the next seven days, her friend Adeline, Lady's maid to the Duchess of Somersby, would soon pay her and Fia a visit. She usually had a frock or two for each of them that were only a couple of years out of fashion. Fashion didn't matter much to Sofie, though Fia might let a few complaints grumble out of her. They weren't complaints so much as observations. Or so Fia always reminded her.

"Sofie, glad you could make an appearance," her father's eyes shone brightly at her. He was truly the most perfect father she could have ever asked for. Even after her mother had passed away, in spite of his grief, he had done his utmost to run the tavern and take care of Sofie the best way he knew how. In fact, there were several ways they honored her mother, Layla, including the placement of a few roses on the walls and in the guest rooms. The red rose was her mother's favorite.

"I'm here for you, Papa." Sofie patted her father's hand and took notice of the extra wrinkles. He had been working a long time at his dream of running the tavern. She only wished he needn't work quite so hard. The tavern was his life, but she wished it didn't have to be his lifeline.

That's why for the last few years she had convinced him to give her some of their profits to invest. And so far she had earned more money than she had lost. Of course, she had to do some wrangling with solicitors and her father any time she wanted to make any changes, but that little hindrance didn't stop Sofie on her quest. It only precipitated more dreams of the day she could have her own bank account and her own full control of her money. As it so happened, this dream was one of the reasons she didn't want to marry, despite having received several offers over the years. Also, every marriage proposal thus far had been prefaced with something akin to, "In light of your great beauty...etcetera etcetera, will you marry me?" She did not want to be someone's trophy. Nor did she want to be anyone's property. In the event she did marry, any authority she might have gained would then transfer over to her husband. And she did not want to have to ask her husband to sign off on every financial decision she made.

And equal to the point, she was more than the beauty men whispered (or spoke loudly) about. She prided herself (though not overly) on her intelligence. Having spent all her spare time, and some working hours, reading all that she could about investments, it was not a pride without foundation. Besides books, if there were any conversations about interest and profit that she could glean wisdom from, she took the time to serve those tables with extra care.

And there were a few patrons who would come in from time to time reliably with interest-full conversations. Lord Reginald was not one of those few, but if he was ever in attendance with the Colonel or any of his duke friends, Sofie served them well. And aside from a recent, but small, incident with Lord Reginald and his friend, the newest Duke of Beauford, every encounter so far had been well-received.

And so it was that if ever a new patron came in talking of investments, Sofie and Fia confirmed with their eyes who would take the table. Because if Sofie could invest and save enough money, she would not only help her father, but of course her best friend as well.

Now, if only she could find a way to attend the Railway Convention happening tomorrow...But that felt like more of a castle in the air dream than a simple castle in the air itself.

Besides the fact that the logistics were a nightmare, there was also the question of how her father would manage in her absence. How would she travel there? How would she gain entrance? Who would go with her? How would she pay for it?

No, it was not meant to be. Castles did not exist in the air. And tavern daughter's did not attend annual Railway Conventions.

Read more.

Read More: The Good Dukes

Turn the page for Chapter 1 of Book 1 in The Good Dukes series: *Good Duke Gone Cold.*

She's a passionate playwright. He's a grumpy, cold duke. And she just needs to resist her desire for him this one summer...

Good Duke Gone Cold

Chapter 1

1815, England

A GIRL NEVER KNOWS where her husband might come from. He could be the neighbor next door. Down the street. He could be her father's friend. A distant cousin twice removed. He could be an earl, a viscount, a prince. He could be the man she just waltzed with or the one waiting behind the fern working up the nerve to ask for the next dance. Or. Or just maybe he could be the clothesless, dripping wet adonis right in front of her.

The memory was so vivid, it felt like he was right in front of her. But where had that memory come from just now? Maybe it was the rain sluicing down the window. That must be it. Mary shook her head. Now was not the time for that memory.

Now was the time to focus on herself and being more than just a woman waiting for a husband. Now was the time to focus on her desires, namely, writing her first play to be performed in front of an audience other than friends and family.

The blank pages rested heavily on her lap. It was strangely warm and comforting, despite its emptiness. This was the year. No, this was the *summer* she would finish this play. It's going to happen. It has to happen. Lady Mary Edwards consoled herself as she brushed a loose cinnamon coloured tendril behind her ear. She would be more than just a woman pursuing fleeting beauty and a faulty husband. There must be more. And this play was it.

Her legs were bent as her back rested against the window frame. She was cozy as her slight frame was hidden behind the drapes. Surrounded by books and feeling the faint flickers from the fire soothed her soul into a state of meditation. This was the place to think. To feel inspired. To express all her pent up passions and let all the words flow into glorious being and insurmountable greatness. To look down at a blank page. Well, yes. All in good time. The play was half written but something was missing. If only she could–

Mary shook her head and peered out the window. She didn't stare at the perfectly manicured trees in the shapes of exotic animals in front of her, or even the fountain full of cherubs. Her mind's eye wandered across the ducal fields of her best friend's family home and onward to her own less opulent estates hidden from view, where neither her father nor mother, in fact no family, was currently in residence. Father and mother had left again. This time to excavate the latest Egyptian treasures. Last time was Morocco. The time before that was Tunisia, or was it India? Every few months took them to a new place with the hollow platitude that she would be fine, if not happier, at her best friend's nearly palatial estates. *Two is more fun than one,* they'd say. *We'll see you soon, have fun with Margaret. Be good. Oh what are we saying, of course you'll be good. Try to keep Margaret in line. Her parents love your influence. See, it's a win-win for everyone.*

Mary didn't mind. Too much. It *was* better with two. And Margaret *was* her best friend. Always had been. Ever since Margaret literally ran into Mary in the fields one day with the biggest grin and wildest eyes she had ever seen. The tenacious memory forced its way back to Mary's mind.

She could still remember the cool breeze on her cheeks. Standing in the middle of a pathway, forgetting to take the next step, she lost her thoughts in the clouds. There were shapes of animals and boats scudding across the sky, morphing into flowers and trees. What made the clouds move? Did others see the same shapes? What would it be like to rest on one of those clouds for a day?

Then, thwack! Something, no, someone, had just run into her shoulder.

Without even taking time to introduce herself, the girl–later found out to be Margaret–yelled, "Run! They're coming!" Mary didn't hesitate. This was not a time to consider the pros and cons or the risks of what might be coming out of the bushes. She picked up her skirts and tried to run after the spritely blonde girl who was still shrieking like a banshee.

Unfortunately, Mary was not made for such impulsive moments as this. Lost in the hysterics, she didn't notice the girl in front of her flinging up an armful of clothing. Instead of the odds of just one item hitting Mary, it seemed like all thirteen items hit her right in the face and caused her to trip over a root and fall face first in the dirt.

Her heart was pounding. She heard footsteps racing toward her. What was coming from behind the hill? How many were there? Who had that girl angered? How angry were they? Mary's palms were clammy. She rolled over, getting tangled in the clothing and was pulling pieces of clothing from her eyes as quickly as she could. And then, in an indelible instant, she wished she could put everything back over her eyes.

Looking up, her eyes beheld the wettest, most heart-throttling sight she had ever seen. Water sluiced down the carefully crafted body right before her eyes. Before her own very eyes.

She should have closed them. She should have put her head back under the loose clothing. Every admonishment and warning ever prevailed upon her reminded her to be genteel. A woman was to be prim and proper, yet every fiber in her body refused to obey. Her eyes took their fill. By Jupiter, he was everything her mind could have thought up to be the embodiment of what a man should be. He lifted one of his large hands to push back his luscious raven hair, just long enough to brush the tops of his ears. The action exposed his thickly arched eyebrows that framed piercing azure eyes, an aquiline nose, and a strong sharp jaw.

Her embarrassingly evident perusal was interrupted with an abrupt demand, "Where is she?" Spoken with such aplomb, Mary hardly believed he knew he had one hand covering his, um, other areas. *Oh did I actually look that far down. It's not possible. I am a lady. Well, ten is almost an adolescent and that's nearly an adult. But I am proper.*

"Uh–"

"You don't look familiar. I suppose you don't even know her, do you? *Her* being Lady Campbell, or Margaret, in light of the forced intimacy of this acquaintance. Well, all in good time. Perhaps you'd like to grace us with our belongings currently entangling you?"

At that moment a second rustling in the bushes and a calm, "Jonathon, just wait there for a moment, please," led her to turn on her stomach and rest her closed eyes on her forearm.

Oh please let this be over soon. Please. Please. Please. Please don't tell my mother and father about this. Just let this be a nightmare.

If only Mary knew what a recurring dream this nightmare would turn into, she might have put a little more effort into listening to those clamoring voices earlier, reminding her to be proper and not continue looking in the first place.

"Well, alright. On your stomach then. If you can't see me, then I'm sure I'm not here. Just stay put. I'll reach around you and grab our clothes. We'll dress quickly and this will all feel like a dream."

Nightmare. Dream. Really, what's the difference besides the untrustworthy emotions they evoke.

***

GREGORY CAMPBELL, DUKE OF Wellingford, stood in the front hall dripping wet from the day's showers. This was home. He should feel comfortable. He should be sauntering in, taking charge, and acting like he owned the place. He did own the place.

At the very least he should be getting changed. But he was frozen in place. As he looked at the front door, he couldn't stop thinking about one of the last times he stared at that same door just after slamming it at his best friend's back. He could still hear the angry shouting.

"You don't know anything, Jonathan. You don't know pain. You don't know the real world. You're just the devil may care, everything will work out guy who doesn't think about anything beyond his next meal or his next lay."

Jonathan, like Gregory, was five-and-twenty at the time. But everything else was unlike Gregory. Where Gregory had turned dark, stern, and mysterious after his father passed away, Jonathan was light and transparent. His shoulders were never burdened like Gregory's, and everything that would have weighed on Gregory rolled right off Jonathan's back. Even his caramel colored hair was cropped shorter and styled asymmetrically, as if he needed more proof of his cavalier approach to life.

Unprovokably, Jonathan's lips curved into a half smile. "Yes. That's right. That's me. That's why we're friends. You keep us from getting into too much trouble, and I keep us from being too dainty."

"Dainty?!" Gregory scoffed. "Is that what you call it? Responsibility? Ownership? To hell with you."

"What are you so riled up about? You know me, I'm always joking around."

"Not everything is always a joke."

"Well, this surely is."

"Right now, your life surely is."

And then, the ever unflappable Jonathan, gave his half smile for the second time, saluted Gregory, and walked out the door.

He walked right out the door, enlisted in the army, and never walked through the doors again. All this, on the anniversary of Gregory's father's death.

"Gregory!" The shout pulled him out of his trance. "My brother, the prodigal in the flesh, has returned! I can't believe you are here. It has been far too long."

"Yes, Margaret. It has been." Margaret, Lady Campbell and her turquoise almond shaped eyes was always sporting a coquettish grin.

She flung her arms around his neck. In fact, come to think of it, Margaret flung many things around, including convention and clothing. His younger sister was overly cheerful, albeit spoiled and somewhat meddling. But her love was always genuine. If not a tad dramatic at times. Women.

Gregory had two rules for women. Keep them happy. And keep them at arm's length.

"–and that is the best part! I'm so happy!" Rule one: check.

"Wonderful. Well, it's good to be home." He turned his head to look back at the door. The distressing memory was like a drain. It was pulling him in so much that he didn't even hear the footsteps and further chatter from Margaret until he felt a light thwump against his chest. Immediately his hands reached down encircling the most perfectly sized-waist. He inhaled a familiar, but exotic, scent of cinnamon and vanilla. The lithe body in his hands was warm and soft, everything he stole his heart against. He felt two pert breasts nuzzled against his chest and then two timid tawny eyes met his.

This was Mary. Margaret's little friend who was not so little anymore. She was a hot blooded grown woman pliable in his hands. He had met Mary when she was ten years old, and she and Margaret had followed him and Jonathan around like lost puppies, until they all became friends of a sort. He recalled teaching her how to fish, ride a horse, and parry a blade. They had always been respectful of each other and had always had innocent fun together. So as his hands melted into her waist after three years of not seeing her, it was uncomfortable to have thoughts enter his mind about what he might teach her as an adult.

What was he thinking? He didn't need this distraction. He came home with a purpose. Everything had to be about the dukedom now. He'd spent enough years wasting his life away on gambling, women, and alcohol. What was it, two? Three? Now it was time to at least have a semblance of control. If not in direct pursuit of cleaning up his reputation, at least to take on responsibilities and not squander the inheritance his ancestors had carefully built and maintained over the last few hundred years.

Hell, this was Chatswick House accommodating 154 bedrooms, 20,000 acres, and hundreds of tenants. There was plenty of work that needed his attention here. His father would be proud that he had finally returned to take his place and start behaving how he had been trained to act. His father was his greatest ally and staunchest supporter. He knew how far to push Gregory. He knew when to hold back and when to unleash. And then in an instant, at sixteen, he was gone. No more strong, unwavering voice reassuring him of his abilities and pushing him to rise to new challenges.

Always a boy with confidence, Gregory had focus and exactitude suited for being a duke. When his father died, he pushed down the hurt, suppressed the uncertainty, and faced his responsibilities with dignity.

Then, when Jonathan went missing at five-and-twenty, Gregory hadn't held it together as well. In fact, he hadn't held it together at all. Now it had been three years since he'd returned, and it was time to come back. It was time to build a home. He had a three step plan: reassess the estates, throw himself into a hobby to avoid close relationships, and secure a wife. Perfectly sound.

Home... Yes, this was the house he grew up in, but it didn't feel like home anymore. He wasn't sure what home was. He knew he needed a roof over his head to protect his body, he knew he needed a hobby for his time and to fill his mind, and he knew he eventually needed an heir for the dukedom to gain his title.

But right here in his hands was someone who used to feel like home. All the memories they shared together threatened to flood his mind, but then, barely beyond a whisper, he heard, "Your Grace."

***

MARY SLOWLY LIFTED HER delicate hands to Gregory's chest to push herself back. It felt like he wasn't letting her go, but that must have been her imagination. Of course, he wasn't holding on to her. Of course, he wasn't holding his breath.

"Isn't that so like me?" Margaret effused. "Here I go attempting the dramatic entrance by twirling our dear, dear friend, and I accidentally overshoot." Margaret chuckled. Her blonde hair glittered in the light, and her shimmering eyes matched the glow. She was effervescence personified. She was the sparkle to Mary's life. They couldn't be more opposite. Where Margaret would run through fields playing pranks on her brother, Mary had been woolgathering lost in the shapes of the clouds. Once the two met, they were inseparable, and Margaret called to the depths of Mary's soul. Margaret knew immediately of Mary's abstract nature and how her creative soul just needed to be prompted out.

That's when the plays began. Mary started writing and couldn't stop. Every few months the girls would be reenacting a new play and dragging Gregory and Jonathan into them, only when the boys were home from Eton, that is. And only when they could be cajoled, threatened, or bribed with baked goods, into participating. When not enacting one of Mary's plays, the girls would follow the older two boys, spying on them to see what mischief they could cause.

Of course, this led the girls into learning quite a few things otherwise unbeknownst to girls: how to swim, fish, fence, ride horses, and even shoot. Summers especially, held the most memories for the girls. It all changed drastically a few years ago when Jonathan went missing. There was one less person laughing.

At this moment though, there was only one person chuckling, and it was about the clumsy introduction she had overshot. Margaret was unaware that she was the only one laughing.

Mary noticed, however. She noticed everything at this particular time and in this particular space, including the solid chest, broad shoulders, and the faint scent of bay rum with a hint of whiskey.

This was a solid chest, even more solid than the last time she was plastered against it. That pesky memory fought its way back to her mind, and Mary was transported back to the day they all met.

"Alright, we're both dressed now. You can stand up and open your eyes." Mary lay still on the ground with her eyes pressed into her forearm.

"You've shocked the poor girl," a second voice cheerfully said. "Here. Let me." The voice belonging to Jonathan approached Mary and tapped her lightly on the shoulder. "Come now. Everything is fine. We'll go find your friend and you two can scamper off and continue whatever other shenanigans you had planned for the day."

Mary didn't feel compelled to correct Jonathan that in fact Margaret wasn't her friend, that she never scampered, and she most definitely never engaged in shenanigans. Instead, she thought maybe joining Margaret was the safer bet.

As she lifted her torso from the ground and began to put weight on her foot to get up, she stumbled. "Ack! I believe I may have twisted my ankle." Jonathan was right there and caught her up and into his arms.

"Ooof! Ok hang on. I've got you." But it did not feel at all like he had her. "Let's be off. Hang on tight." And he started to amble down the pathway in hopes of meeting up with Margaret. Mary's head bumped against his chest and her arms were uncomfortably settled on her stomach. Just then, Jonathan tripped and lurched forward. Mary grasped for his neck as he recovered his footing. This did not feel safe at all.

"Darn roots! If I can stumble, being as athletic as I am, I see how anyone could have done so just as easily." His chuckle lightened the mood and put Mary at ease for her earlier stumble, but she was unassured of her current level of safety in his arms.

"Give the chit to me before you break her neck," Gregory demanded with a scowl.

"I'm not a chit! And I'm not just some piece of–" before she could finish Jonathan handed her off Gregory.

"She's all yours! I'm going to find Margaret and give her something to think about." With that he laughed and ran off leaving Mary in Gregory's strong, capable arms, and resting against his solid, warm chest. It was safe, and it felt like home.

That was the moment she fell in love with him.

That solid, warm chest was the same solid, warm chest that she was now resting against. She pulled her mind to the present and pushed herself away from home.

His harsh, cold voice doused her heart with ice water, "Lady Mary."

Read more.

Made in the USA
Middletown, DE
21 January 2024